I'm Going To READ!™

These levels are mea[...]
you and your child can best [...]

UP TO 50 WORDS

Level 1: Kinderg[...] Grade 1 . . . Ages 4–6
- word bank to highlight new words
- consistent placement of text to promote readability
- easy words and phrases
- simple sentences build to make simple stories
- art and design help new readers decode text

UP TO 100 WORDS

Level 2: Grade 1 . . . Ages 6–7
- word bank to highlight new words
- rhyming texts introduced
- more difficult words, but vocabulary is still limited
- longer sentences and longer stories
- designed for easy readability

UP TO 200 WORDS

Level 3: Grade 2 . . . Ages 7–8
- richer vocabulary of up to 200 different words
- varied sentence structure
- high-interest stories with longer plots
- designed to promote independent reading

MORE THAN 300 WORDS

Level 4: Grades 3 and up . . . Ages 8 and up
- richer vocabulary of more than 300 different words
- short chapters, multiple stories, or poems
- more complex plots for the newly independent reader
- emphasis on reading for meaning

LEVEL 2

Library of Congress Cataloging-in-Publication Data Available

2 4 6 8 10 9 7 5 3 1

Published by Sterling Publishing Co., Inc.
387 Park Avenue South, New York, NY 10016
Text © 2006 by Harriet Ziefert Inc.
Illustrations © 2006 by Pete Whitehead
Distributed in Canada by Sterling Publishing
c/o Canadian Manda Group, 165 Dufferin Street,
Toronto, Ontario, Canada M6K 3H6
Distributed in the United Kingdom by GMC Distribution Services,
Castle Place, 166 High Street, Lewes, East Sussex, England BN7 1XU
Distributed in Australia by Capricorn Link (Australia) Pty. Ltd.
P.O. Box 704, Windsor, NSW 2756, Australia

I'm Going To Read is a trademark of Sterling Publishing Co., Inc.

Printed in China

Sterling ISBN-13: 978-1-4027-3418-2
ISBN-10: 1-4027-3418-2

For information about custom editions, special sales, premium and
corporate purchases, please contact Sterling Special Sales
Department at 800-805-5489 or specialsales@sterlingpub.com.

HUNGRY DINOSAUR

Pictures by Pete Whitehead

Sterling Publishing Co., Inc.
New York

The dinosaur walked—
thump! thump!

"I'm hungry,"
he said to a **parrot**.
"And I eat **pa . . .**"

won't · me · you · don't

"Please!" cried the parrot.
"Please don't eat me!"

"**Parrot**, I won't eat you.
I eat **papaya**!"

The dinosaur walked—
thump! thump!

"I'm so hungry,"
he said to a **pig**.
"And I eat **pi** . . ."

"Please!" cried the pig.
"Don't eat me!"

"**Pig**, I won't eat you.
I eat **pickles!**"

The dinosaur walked—
thump! thump!

"I'm so hungry,"
he said to a **puppy**.
"And I eat **pu** . . ."

"Please," cried the puppy.
"Don't eat me."

"**Puppy**, I won't eat you.
I eat **pumpkins**!"

The dinosaur walked—
thump! thump!

"I'm so, so hungry,"
he said to some **people**.
"And I eat **pe** . . . "

"**Peaches**?" they asked.

"Come with us."

"I'll come," said the dinosaur.

They went to a store.

"I'm so hungry,"
said the dinosaur.
"So hungry!"

They fed the dinosaur
papaya, pickles,
pumpkin, and peaches.

"Yummy!" said the dinosaur.
"I like papaya.

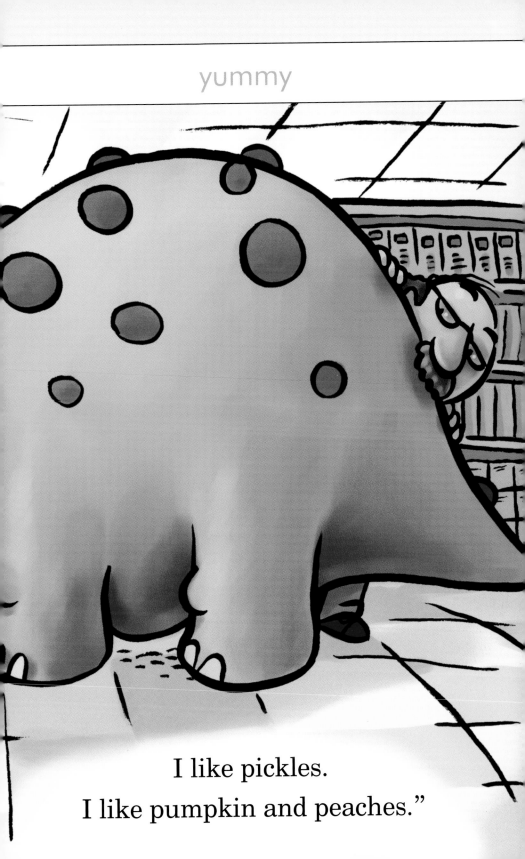

yummy

I like pickles.
I like pumpkin and peaches."

"But I'm still hungry.
So hungry!"

"Do you want a hot dog?"
asked the girl.

"I want a plant,"
said the dinosaur.

"I like plants."

"I'm an Apatosaurus.
No meat for me!"